"This book is dedicated to my grandchildren,
Riley, Dylan and Jake. With love."

Everything at the farm was going beautifully when Mamma
Mouse got a birdogram. "A message from the sky! Oh my!"
said Mamma Mouse.

"Our cousins from San Francisco are coming to visit us."

Her children, Tommy and Tammy, love the outdoors and were in the swimming pool.

Before you could say "cheese," both Tommy and Tammy jumped up and said, "Look, they're here. Our cousins from San Francisco! They're here!"

"Thank you," said cousin Pete. "Come up, come in," said Papa Mouse, as they climbed up the comb ladder into the hollow cinder blocks they called home.

Excitement was everywhere, as cousins, Pete and Polly Mouse and their children, Matt and Molly arrived. "Welcome to our humble abode," smiled Mamma Mouse.

"Our long trip has made us very hungry," said Pete.
"Good," said Mamma Mouse, as she loosened kernels of corn from the cob with a wheat stalk.
"Dinner is served." Each mouse got his own kernel to dip into the sewing thimble full of butter. Matt and Molly took lots.
"Well," said a shocked Polly, "I never".
 "Oh, I bet you have!" laughed Papa Mouse.

After dinner the children enjoyed fresh raspberries right off the bush.

"Oh Good heavens, look! They're covered
with raspberry juice!" said a distressed Polly.
"Oh, let them be, they're having fun, like we
did when we were young," said Papa Mouse.

"Oh cousins," moaned Polly, "How can you live like this? Life on a farm is so hard! You're missing the finer things of life! You should come and live with us in San Francisco." "Oh my, can we?" said the red-mouthed Tommy and Tammy. "We love our San Francisco cousins and I've never been there," said an enthusiastic Mamma Mouse, as she wiped off raspberry juice. Papa mouse nodded, "Yes!" The children cheered, "Hooray!"

With all the excitement, the mice slept very well.
The next day, they got up at the crack of dawn to
see a beautiful sunrise. Mama Mouse asked
Mrs. Chicken for an egg,
and Mrs. Cow for milk.

Just then, Sam Squirrel stopped by and invited everyone
for a ride on his tail. Papa Mouse thought that was a great
idea, and before you could say "Cheddar cheese," the mice
leapt on Sam's bushy tail.
Oh, the Squeals of joy, as he bounced over hill and dale.
Thank goodness squirrels have bushy tails, the mice had
something to grab onto! Riding Sam's tail was like being
on a fun ride at Disneyland.

The trip was so much fun. Everyone sang songs all the way, "eight-mouse harmony." Glorious!

When they arrived, Polly
led them all into the basement.

"After you," said Pete, as they all piled into a large contraption.

"What is this thing?" said Mamma.

"An elevator," said Pete. "It's going to take us to our penthouse apartment."

Suddenly it started and moved up, up, up, and finally stopped at the penthouse. "Oh my," said Mamma, "just as smooth as can be. Everybody off!"

So, everybody got off, and they made their way into the penthouse. "Welcome to our home!" said Polly. "How about a refreshing bubble bath?"

"How posh!" said Mamma. "Wow wee!" said Tommy and Tammy.

"That's imported Swiss cheese, Crepe Suzettes, real whipped cream, and, of course, Russian caviar," said Pete.

"Wow wee! We're eatin' good now!" shouted Tammy, as she tasted the caviar. "Oh! Phew Phew!"said Tammy, spitting it out.
"Hah hah, no one likes caviar at first," laughed Polly. "You have to acquire a taste, don't you know?"

"And these?" asked Tommy.
"Those are chocolate covered strawberries," gloated Polly. "Enjoy!"
"Well, I never!" said Mamma.
"Bet you have!" quipped Pete.
Papa laughed out loud. All the mice squealed with delight.

Suddenly, a giant Angora cat appeared from nowhere. "Run!" said Pete. "Make haste!" yelled Polly. The giant cat hissed and growled. "Oh Mama!" said Papa. "Holey Swiss Cheese!" screamed the kids. "SNARL!" said the giant cat. "Oh dear!" said Mama. "Lets get outta here!" yelled Tommy and Tammy.

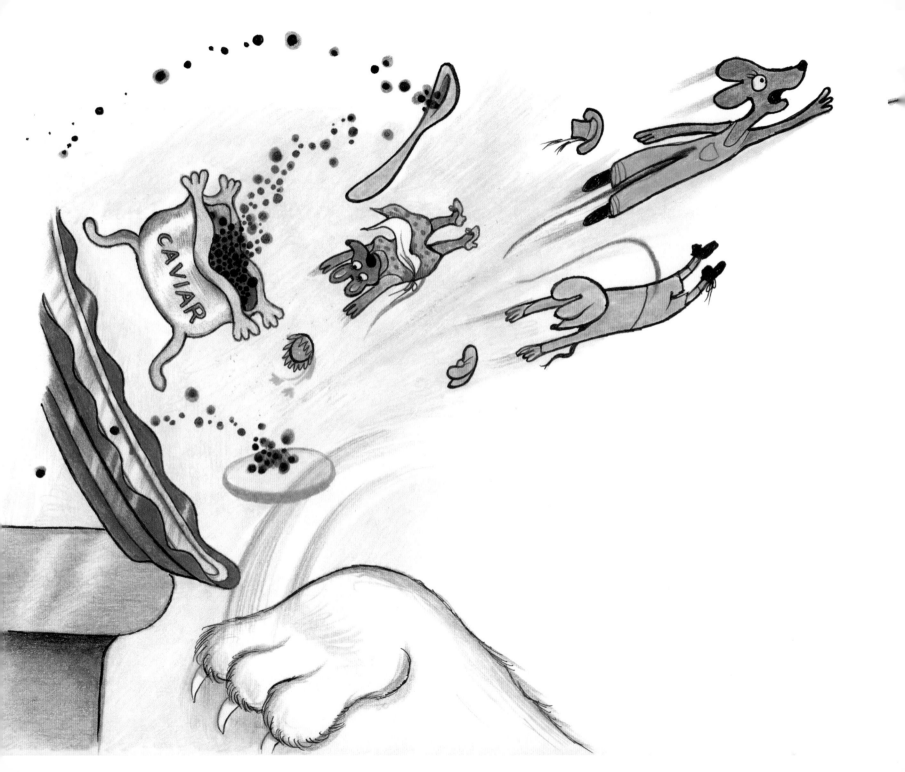

The excited cat pounced, hitting the tray and, horrors, up it sprang, sending mice flying through the air. What a sight! They looked like those flying acrobats from the circus.

Landing on the drapes, the mice clung on for dear life. The giant cat was after them in hot pursuit, shredding the drapes as she climbed closer to the frightened mice, who looked down in horror! Tommy yelled, "Papa, I'm not having a good time. I want to go home!" "Me too," said Papa. "Oh," cried Mama. "Jeepers, creepers!"

Trembling with fear at the top of the drapes, the mice were trying to catch their breath. "My goodness," said Mama, "that is the biggest cat I ever saw." "Ow!" said Tommy, bending over. "What is it?" said Mama. "My tummy hurts," moaned Tommy. "No wonder, with all that rich food," said Mama, as she rubbed his tummy.

Then, as if by magic, the lady of the house appeared, swinging a large broom. She shouted, "Cleopatra, you naughty cat! My new drapes-ruined. Go on, Cleo, scat!" And...scat she did! "Well, good riddance!"

The relieved mice crawled down from the
drapes. Papa said, "I think we've had
enough of this place! Let's go home!"
Mama said, "Okey dokey."

Mama, Papa, Tommy and Tammy were so happy to see their "Home Sweet Home."

That night, enjoying their simple country life, everyone agreed, there's no place like home.

Graphic design and layout by
John Villegas

DOM DeLUISE

NO Place Like HOME Recipes

DEAR PARENTS,
YOUNG CHILDREN SHOULD NEVER COOK BY THEMSELVES,
HOWEVER, YOU MIGHT ENJOY HELPING THEM PREPARE SOME OF
THESE TASTY DISHES.

Mamma's
Scrambled Eggs with Cheese

1tbs	butter or margarine
3-4	eggs
1oz	milk
2 slices	American cheese
	salt & pepper, to taste

Break eggs into bowl. Add milk, salt & pepper, beat with a fork.

In a nonstick pan, heat butter until melted. Add eggs to pan. Add cheese. Use a wooden spoon to slowly move eggs around in the pan, until they are done, but moist.

Serve on a plate with tomato slices, bacon, sausage, or a dollop of cottage cheese.

Serve with toast and butter or jam. Serves 2.

Polly's
Chocolate Dipped Strawberries

a dozen or so strawberries
3-4 milk chocolate candy bars

Put bars in a *double broiler or microwave in a bowl for about 1 1/2 minutes, until fully melted.
Hold stem of strawberry and dip halfway into bowl of chocolate.
Place on a tray. Refrigerate.
Serve cold as a finger-food desert.
* (a pot within a pot with water, or "water bath")

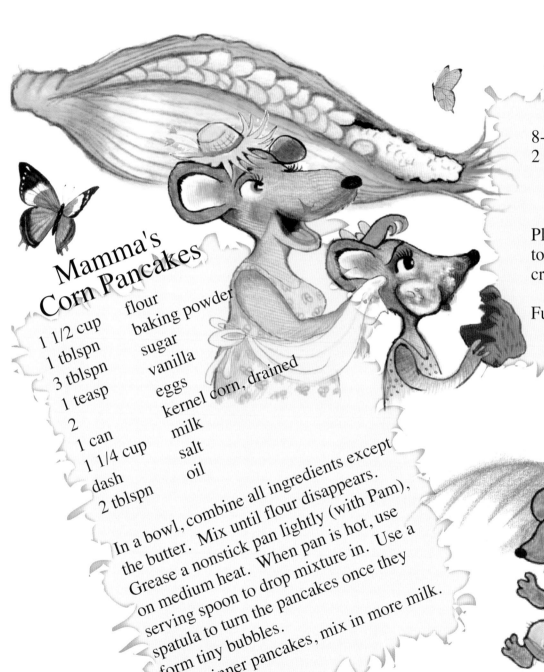

Tammy's Raspberry A La Mode

8-10	fresh raspberries
2 scoops	vanilla ice-cream
	whipped cream

Place the ice-cream in a small desert dish, top with fresh raspberries and whipped cream.

Fun and delicious!

Mamma's Corn Pancakes

1 1/2 cup	flour
1 tblspn	baking powder
3 tblspn	sugar
1 teasp	vanilla
2	eggs
1 can	kernel corn, drained
1 1/4 cup	milk
dash	salt
2 tblspn	oil

In a bowl, combine all ingredients except the butter. Mix until flour disappears. Grease a nonstick pan lightly (with Pam), on medium heat. When pan is hot, use serving spoon to drop mixture in. Use a spatula to turn the pancakes once they form tiny bubbles. For thinner pancakes, mix in more milk.
Serves 4-6.

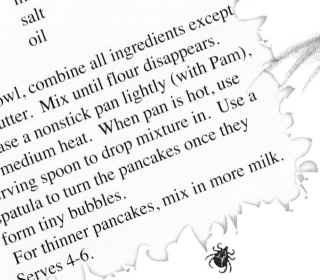

DOM DeLUISE

Dom Deluise is a comedian-actor-writer who lives in Los Angeles. His children's books include "Charlie the Caterpillar," "King Bob's New Clothes," "Goldilocks," "Hansel and Gretel," "The Nightingale" and "The Pouch Potato." Dom has written two cookbooks, "Eat This" and "Eat This Too." Dom's happiest when he's working with his wife, Carol, on such productions as Peter, Michael and David, and their three grandchildren, Riley, Dylan and Jake! Dom and Carol are very proud of all of them.

no Place Like HOME

After leaving "Loretto Heights College" in Denver, Tim Brown had a stint at American Music and Dramatic Academy in Manhattan.

He began as an illustrator with his friend Dom with "No Place Like Home". Tim makes his home in Los Angeles. His work has been published in magazines across the country. He is looking forward to his next project, with, hopefully, less mice!

Illustrated By

TIM BROWN

www.domdeluise.com

NOTES

_____

_____

_____

_____

_____

_____

                        _____

                        _____

                        _____

                        _____

                        _____

                        _____

                        _____

NOTES

_____

_____

_____

_____

_____

_____

_____

_____

_____

_____

_____

_____